STAR CROSSED

Julia Denos

HOUGHTON MIFFLIN HARCOURT | Boston   New York

For the Boggies, long-distance
friends from the stars

All rights reserved. For information about permission to reproduce selections from this book,
write to trade.permissions@hmhco.com or to Permissions, Houghton Mifflin Harcourt Publishing Company,
3 Park Avenue, 19th Floor, New York, New York 10016.

hmhbooks.com

The illustrations in this book were done in watercolor, India ink, salt, graphite, pastels, and digital paint.
The text type and display type were set in Centaur MT.

Designed by Whitney Leader-Picone

Library of Congress Cataloging-in-Publication Data is on file.

ISBN: 978-0-358-15395-5

Manufactured in China
SCP 10 9 8 7 6 5 4 3 2 1
4500800955

It was a time when there were still students of the stars.

Eridani was one of them.

He was more of a constellation than a boy.

She was made of
blood and bones,

and he was made of
space and stars.

And even though they lived pretty far
apart, they were best friends.

At the end of each day, Acamar would call
to her, over the sunset:

HEY, ERi, CAN
YOU SEE ME YET?

Eridani would shout into the sky:

ALMOST!

Eridani was always looking up,
out any window she could.

Her eyes were always full of stars.
It was how they met in the first place.

Looking up so much made her good at sky maps and
star plots, so Professor Lunarius put Eridani in charge
of the most important celestial projects at school.

Every evening, after lessons, the students
would walk back to their homes in pairs.
Except for Eridani. She walked alone, but
she wasn't *really* alone.

"How was class?" Acamar asked her one
night, doing somersaults over a moon.
"Good," said Eridani into the sky.
"But I still want to know more."

LiKe WHat?

asked Acamar.

Like:
How Ancient are the STARS?
And how Deep is space, or does it go on FOREVER?
How do Comets Feel?
They tickle.

Eridani laughed.
Acamar smiled.
Then *he* had a question.

ERi, what's
SUNSet Like?

Eridani's heart fell, knowing
Acamar would love sunset, but
he would never get to see one.

She changed the subject.

What's flying like?

Acamar's stars dimmed,
knowing Eridani would
love flying, but she would
never get the chance.
He changed the subject, too.

"Want to race the rest of the way?" Acamar asked
like always.
But this time, he felt too far.
He wanted to be down in the sand.
"Okay," said Eridani, but this time, her feet felt
too heavy.
She wanted to be up in the stars.

Acamar looked down at the stars in his body
and offered them to her.
"You can wish on me, if you want," he said.

"Thanks," said Eridani, choosing a bright one near his heart.

She wished she could return the favor. She wished they could wish together.

"Can't you wish, Acamar?"

"I'm not sure," said Acamar.

He'd never thought of trying to wish, until now. There were Eridani's eyes, so full of stars . . . He chose a bright one, right before she closed them.

Then Eridani wished on Acamar.

And Acamar wished on Eridani.

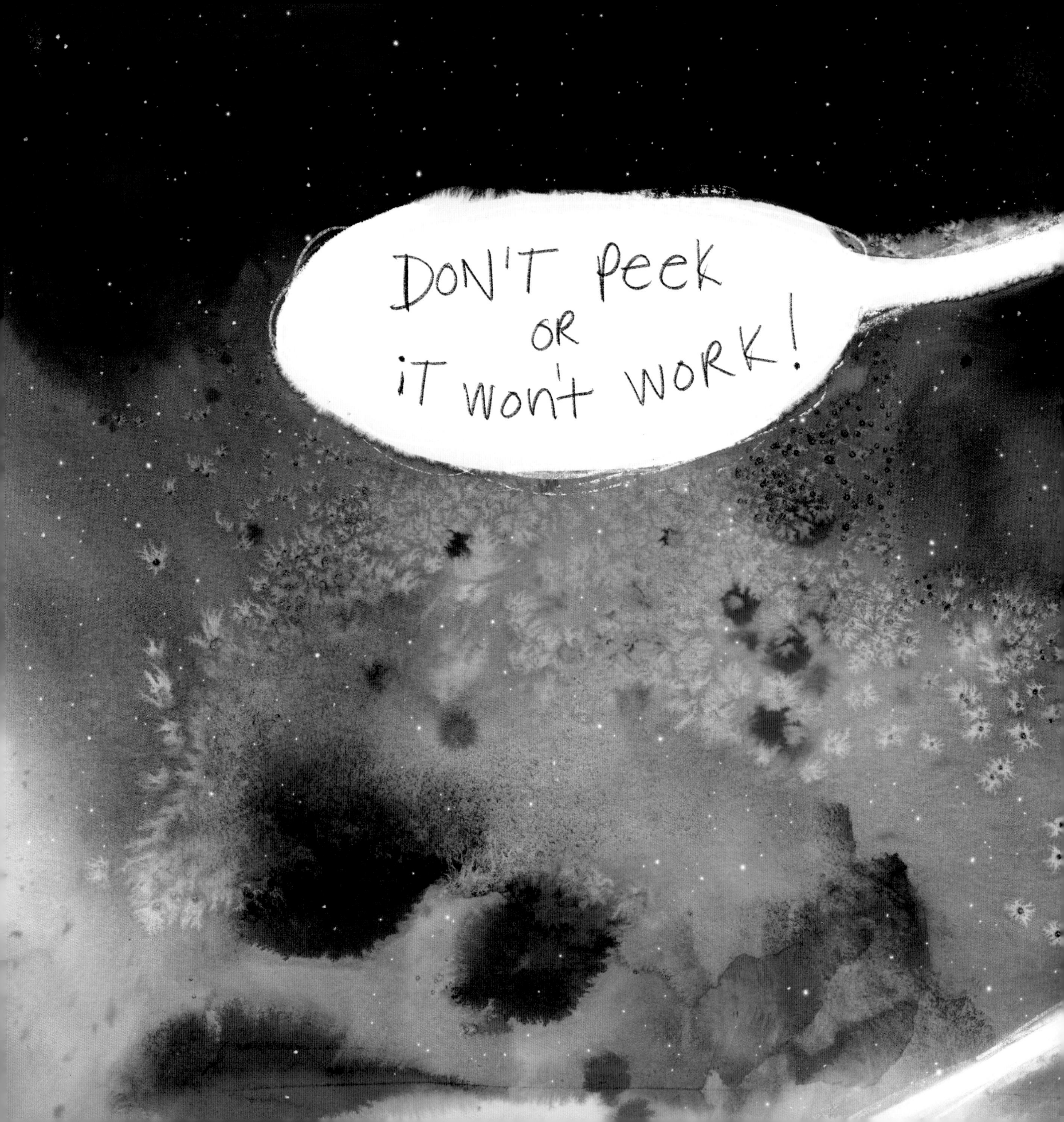
DON'T Peek OR iT won't WORK!

It worked!

Sparks tickled in Eridani's skin. Space shimmered blue under her fingernails. Her bones dissolved into stardust as her body filled with light.

WHOAAAAAAA!!

It will be the best surprise! they thought at the same time, as they flickered through the night with their eyes closed.

Weeeeee!!

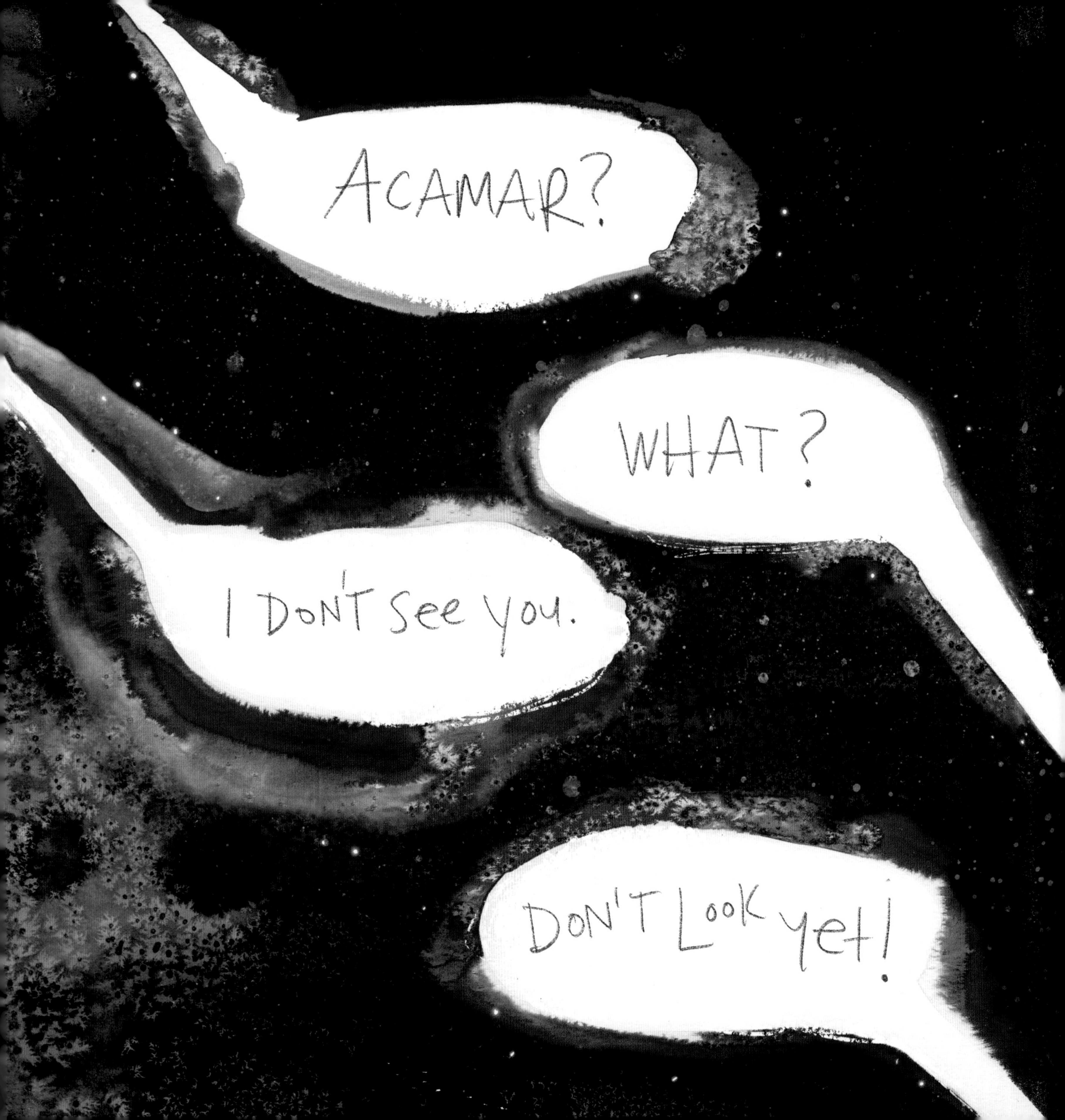
ACAMAR?
WHAT?
I DON'T See you.
DON'T LOOK yet!

Eridani couldn't help but look. She could see that her friend was not in his usual place. The sky was empty where he had just been.

ACAMAR!

Acamar was too busy to answer her—he was watching his blood and bones appear. He was watching the rivers and sands grow wider, the lights of Eridani's city grow warmer, and the window where she slept grow closer and closer.

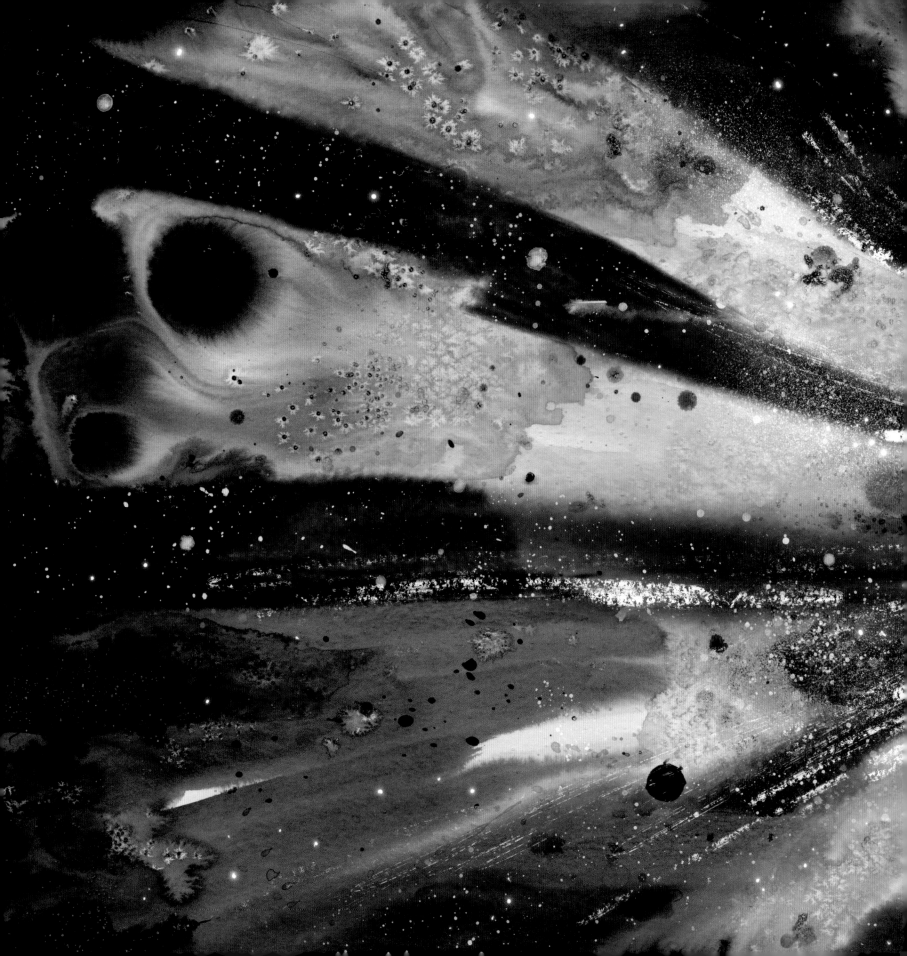

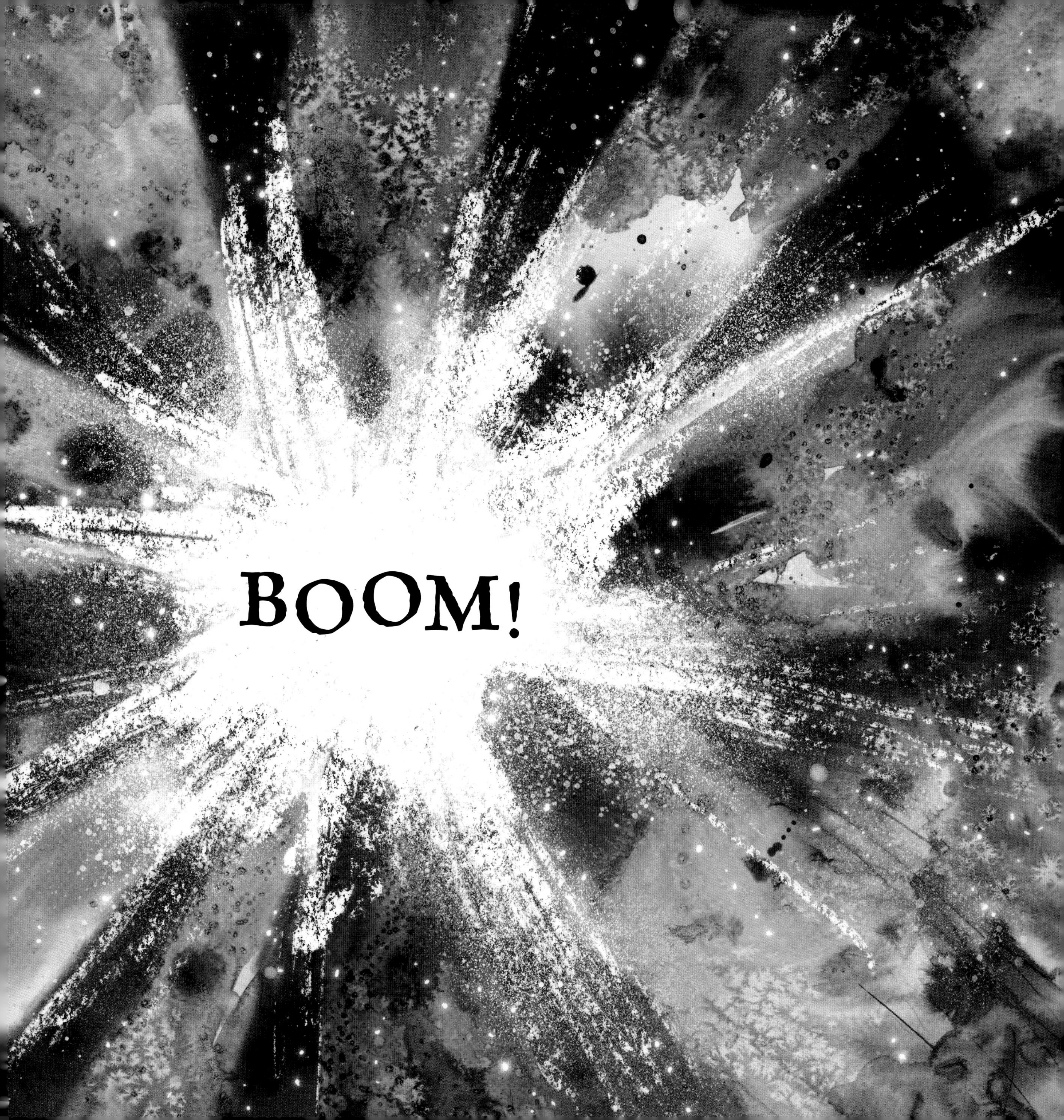

BOOM!

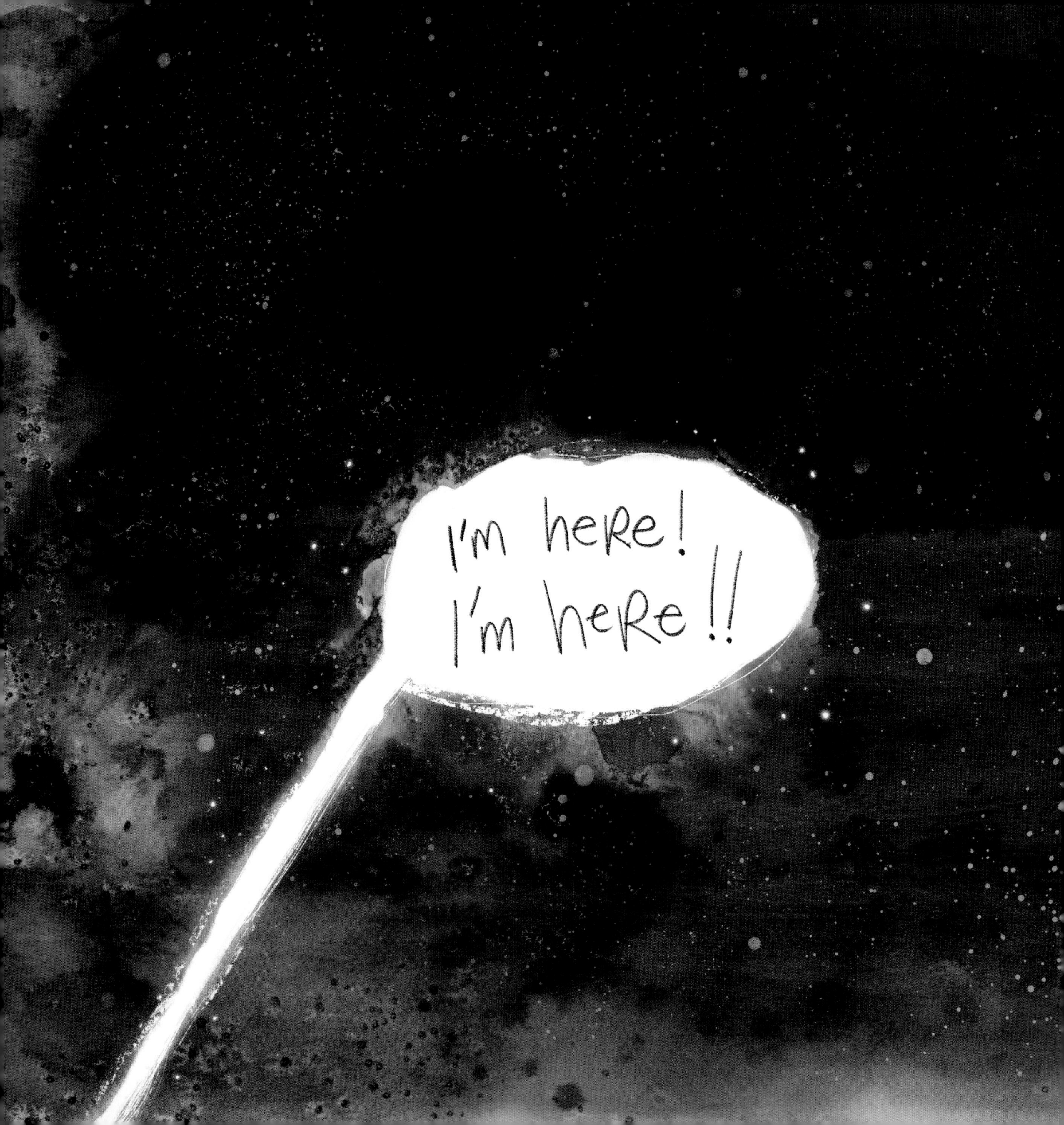
I'm here! I'm here!!

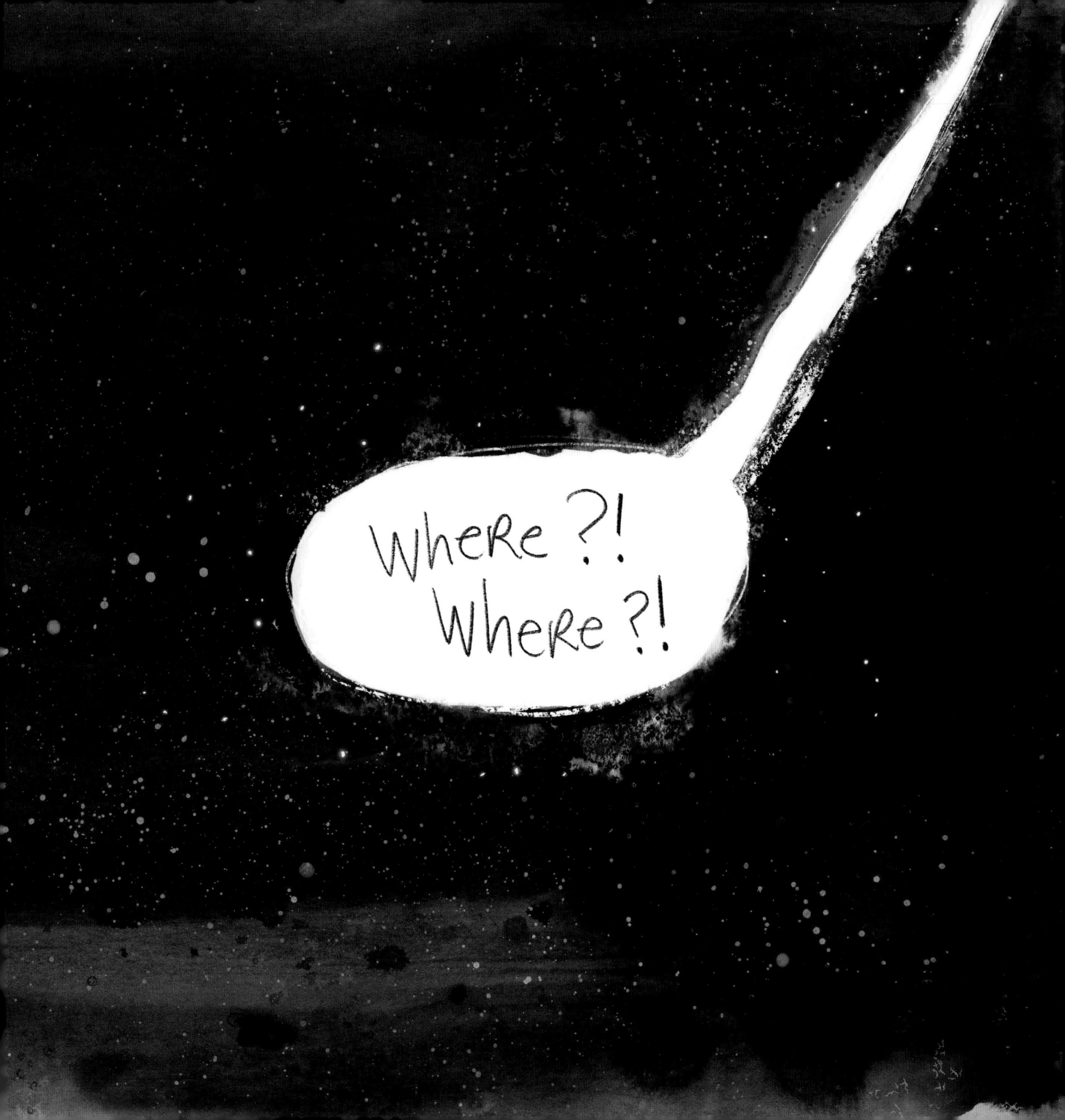
Where?! Where?!

Acamar looked up. There were the stars
in the dome of the sky. There was a new
constellation where *he* had just been.
There was . . .

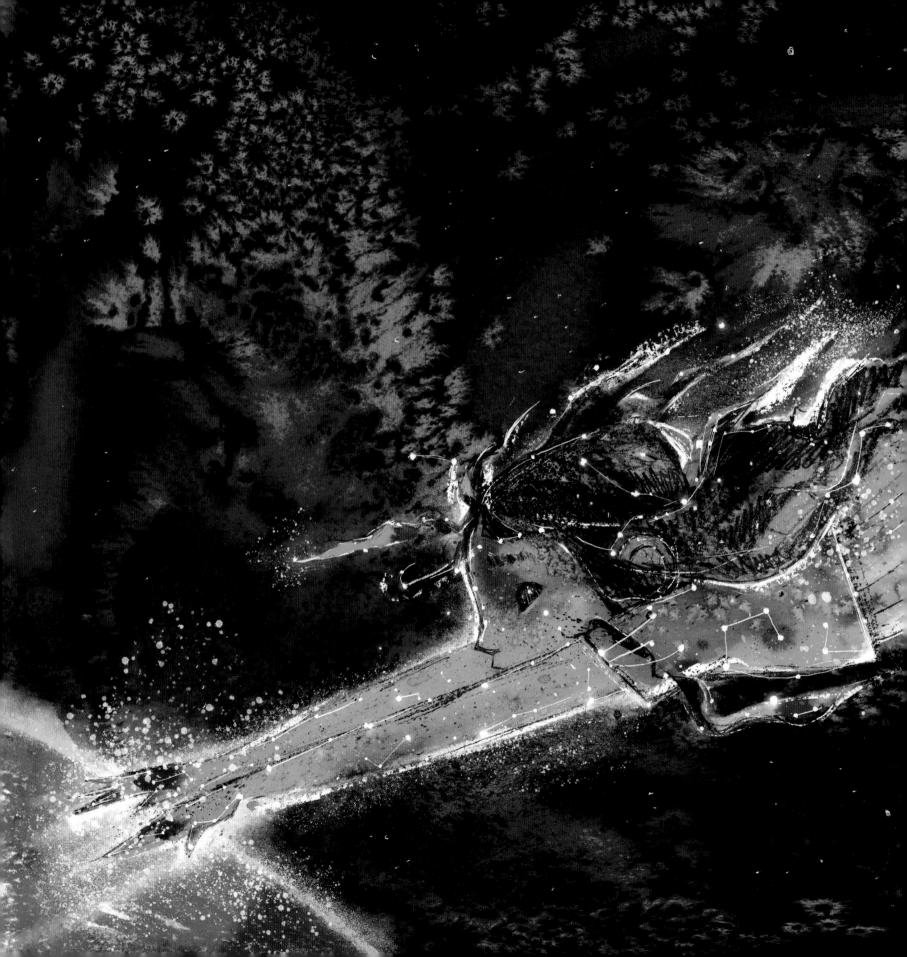

Eridani heard his voice through the misty
atmosphere of the planet she had just
left. She followed his light past familiar
constellations, backwards and downward.
There was Acamar, as bright as ever.

"How did you get way up there?"
asked Acamar.

"I wished!" Eridani answered.

"For what?" asked Acamar.

"To be where *you* are," answered
Eridani.

"Oh," Acamar replied. "Me too."

Space settled sadly between them again.

For a moment, they felt sorry for themselves, and for their spent wishes.

"Well, it worked," said Eridani, shivering.

"Always does," said Acamar, walking away from his crater.

"It's different . . . but the same," said Eridani.

"We're still apart."

Then a comet zoomed across her nose.

"That tickles!"

"I told you!"

Eridani laughed.

Acamar smiled.

Eridani's shiver became a shimmer.

It felt good to shimmer.

Acamar let his new toes sink into the soft sand.

It felt good to sink.

"It's like home," said Eridani, among the stars she loved.

"Yeah," said Acamar, enjoying the night air on his new skin. "But I wish I could see you better. Eyes don't reach very far."

He looked up at his friend. She was just a few dots in the sky now.

"You can have my skyglass!" cried Eridani,
flying over the desert.

"Why don't you go to school tomorrow?
I left it on my desk."

The next evening, Acamar put sandals on.

It felt wonderful to have feet.

He used them to walk into his first sunset, following
the path he'd seen Eridani take every day to school.
She called to him from behind the glow.

When he arrived at the observatory, the classroom was echoing with excitement.

"A shooting star last night, class! AND a new constellation in the sky! We need every student on task!" rang Professor Lunarius. "Where is Eridani?"

Acamar stepped carefully from the shadows.

"Maybe I can help," he said.

The professor studied him through her glasses.

"Who are YOU?"

"My name is Acamar."

"Acamar, what do YOU know about stars?"

Eridani laughed.

Acamar smiled.

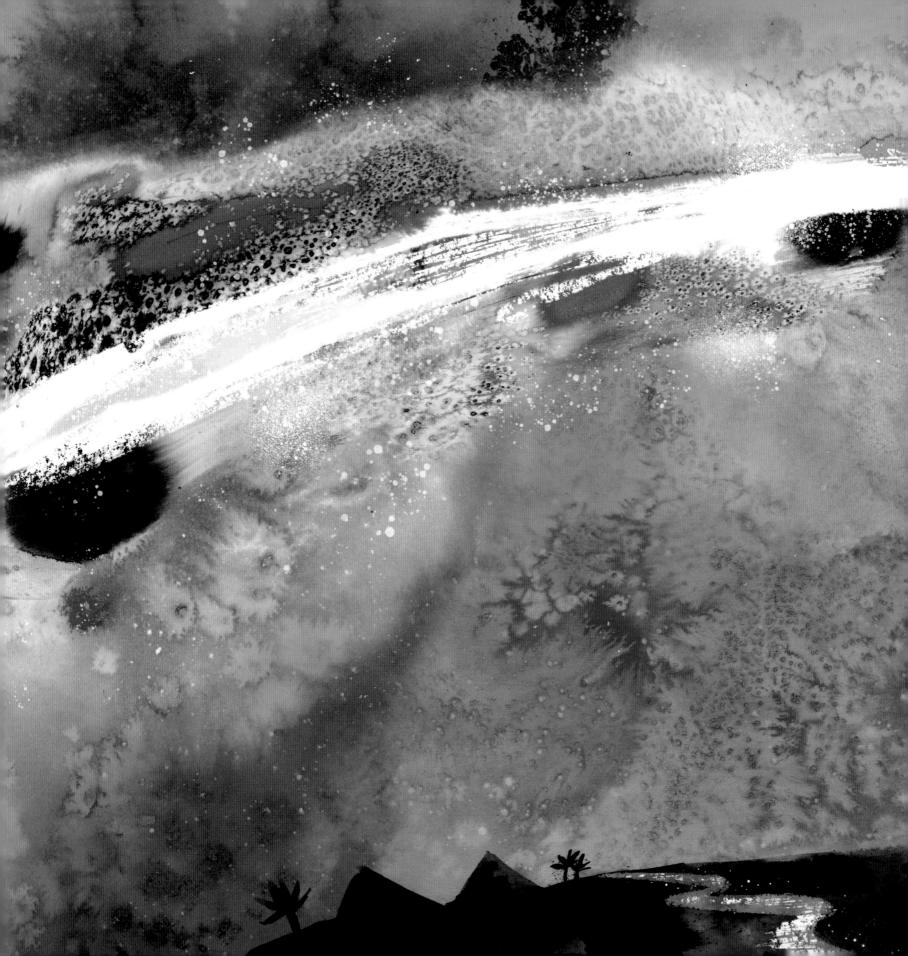

Author's Note

Deep in our night sky, there is a real constellation of stars called Eridanus. It is situated amongst its neighbors, Orion, Fornax, and Taurus. Eridanus is also known as "The River." In ancient times, the brightest star in Eridanus was called "Acamar" or "The End of the River." Acamar is actually a *binary star*, which means that although it appears as a single point of light to our eyes, when we use a strong telescope, we discover a secret: Acamar is made of *two* stars! Astronomers call them Theta-1 Eri and Theta-2 Eri.

These companion stars, two friends in orbit, are gravitationally bound to one another—not touching, yet making a singular, brilliant light. Their positioning also allows them to work together as a team; binary star systems can create supernovas, black holes, and even new planets. This special connection inspired me to tell the story of Acamar and Eridani's long-distance friendship, which reminds us that sometimes space and time are perfectly arranged for magic to occur.

If you'd like to learn more about stars and constellations, here are ways to begin:

Download, print, and make your own star finder.
spaceplace.nasa.gov/starfinder

Find a planetarium.
www.go-astronomy.com/planetariums.htm

Find a dark sky park.
www.darksky.org

Visit your local library.

Look up! I'll be looking up with you.

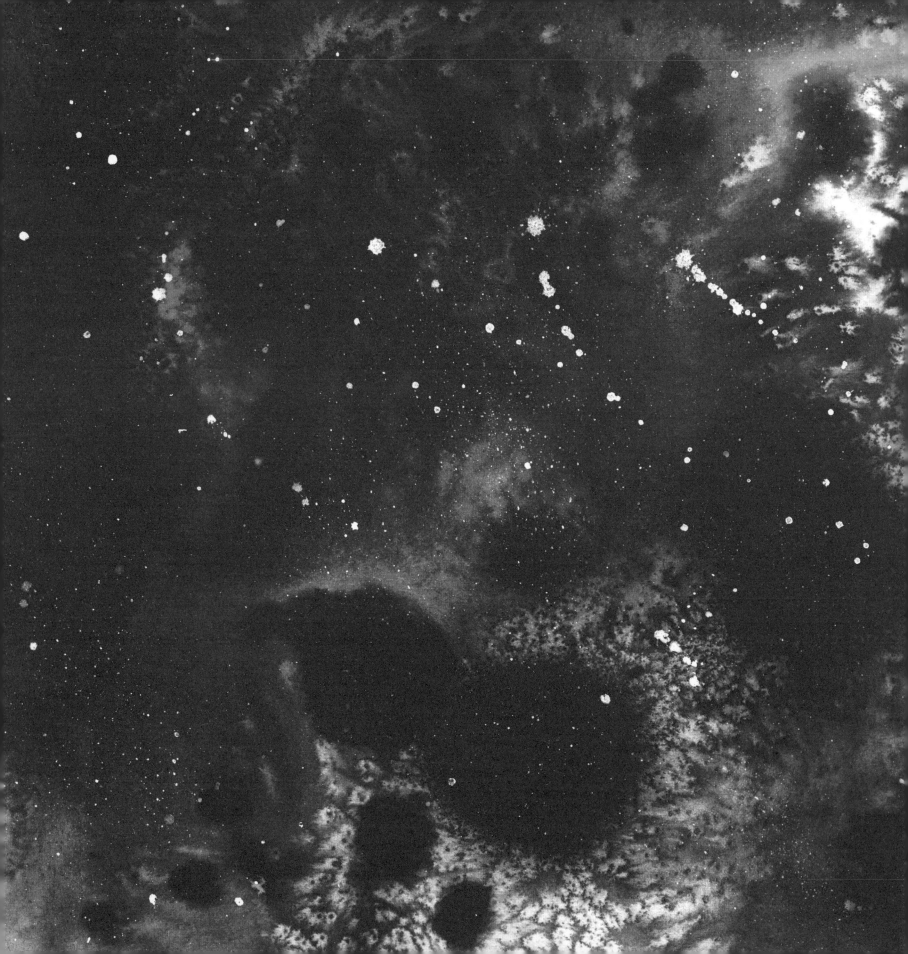